Better Than Home

An Ivy and Mack story

Written by Rebecca Colby

Illustrated by Gustavo Mazali

with Dusan Pavlic

Collins

What's in this story?

Listen and say 

 Download the audio at www.collins.co.uk/839804

forest
waterfall

It was holiday time! Ivy and Mack brought their bags out to the car.

"Is the camera in the car?" asked Ivy. "I need it for my summer homework."

"Yes, Ivy. Have you got everything, Mack?" asked Dad.

Mack ran back to the house. He wanted Croc to come on holiday, too.

Ivy and Mack looked out the window.

Mum and Dad showed Ivy and Mack their holiday home.

"This is our new home for the week," said Dad.

"It's *better* than home!" said Mack.

There were lots of things to do at the holiday park.

They had breakfast in the garden.

They played table tennis.

And they played badminton.

Mack and Dad swam in the pool and Ivy took photos.

"You're fast," said Dad.

"You're faster," said Mack.

"Smile, please!" said Ivy.

One day, they went for a bike ride in the forest. They saw a mountain.

“Look at that mountain!” said Mack. “Can we climb it?”

“Can we stop and take photos for school?” asked Ivy.

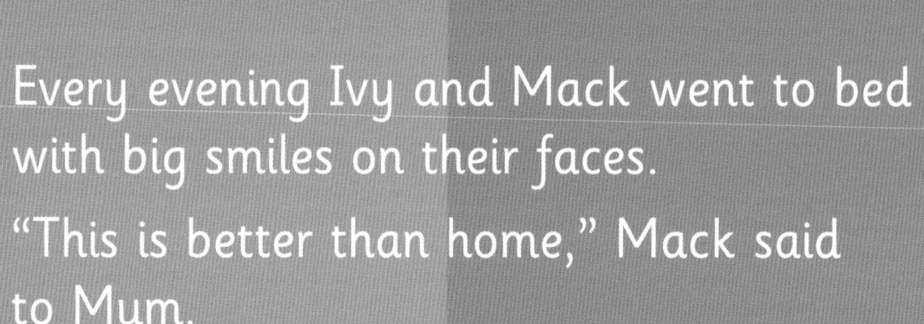

Every evening Ivy and Mack went to bed with big smiles on their faces.

"This is better than home," Mack said to Mum.

"Yes, it is," said Ivy.

One day, they went for a very long walk.
Dad carried the picnic lunch.

"Let's play *king of the mountain*," said Mack.

Ivy took lots of photos.
“These trees are fantastic!” said Ivy.
“I like climbing on the rocks,” said Mack.
“I like the flowers,” said Mum.
“I’d like lunch,” said Dad.
Ivy and Mack laughed.

Mack ran to the top. “I did it! I’m the king of the mountain!”

“Who wants a sandwich?” asked Dad.

The family walked down the mountain.

"This isn't right," said Mum.

"Let's go back," said Ivy.

They came to a waterfall.

“Wow!” said Ivy. “That’s beautiful!” She took a photo.

“I don’t remember a waterfall!” said Mum.

“Which way?” asked Dad.

They walked and they walked. But then they saw the waterfall again.

“Oh dear!” said Mum. “We walked in a big circle.”

“My legs are tired,” said Ivy.

“Can we sleep here?” asked Mack.

“NO!” said Mum and Dad.

They walked again. Then Ivy had a good idea.

"We can look at my photos," she said. "They can show us where to go."

Ivy looked at each photo and saw the right way to go.

"This path takes us to the holiday home!" said Ivy.

"Well done, Ivy," said Mum. "There are the flowers!"

"And the rocks," said Mack.

"And the trees," said Dad.

Back at home, Ivy and Mack talked about their holiday.

"I loved our holiday," said Mack. "Sometimes a holiday is better than home …"

Ivy thought about the holiday. She looked at the garden. There were lots of flowers and trees there too. Mum and Dad smiled.

Ivy said, “And sometimes home is the best place of all!”

Picture dictionary

Listen and repeat 

badminton

bike ride

camera

holiday home

swim

table tennis

1 Look and order the story

2 Listen and say 

Download a reading guide for parents and teachers at
www.collins.co.uk/839804

Collins

Published by Collins
An imprint of HarperCollins*Publishers*
Westerhill Road
Bishopbriggs
Glasgow
G64 2QT

HarperCollins*Publishers*
1st Floor, Watermarque Building
Ringsend Road
Dublin 4
Ireland

William Collins' dream of knowledge for all began with the publication of his first book in 1819.

A self-educated mill worker, he not only enriched millions of lives, but also founded a flourishing publishing house. Today, staying true to this spirit, Collins books are packed with inspiration, innovation and practical expertise. They place you at the centre of a world of possibility and give you exactly what you need to explore it.

10 9 8 7 6 5 4 3 2

ISBN 978-0-00-839804-0

www.collins.co.uk/elt

British Library Cataloguing in Publication Data

A catalogue record for this publication is available from the British Library.

Author: Rebecca Colby
Lead illustrator: Gustavo Mazali (Beehive)
Copy illustrator: Dusan Pavlic (Beehive)
Series editor: Rebecca Adlard
Commissioning editor: Zoë Clarke
Publishing manager: Lisa Todd
Product managers: Jennifer Hall and Caroline Green
In-house editor: Alma Puts Keren
Project manager: Emily Hooton
Editor: Deborah Friedland
Proofreaders: Natalie Murray and Michael Lamb
Cover designer: Kevin Robbins
Typesetter: 2Hoots Publishing Services Ltd
Audio produced by id audio, London
Reading guide author: Julie Penn
Production controller: Rachel Weaver
Printed and bound by: GPS Group, Slovenia

MIX
Paper from responsible sources
FSC™ C007454

This book is produced from independently certified FSC™ paper to ensure responsible forest management.

For more information visit: **www.harpercollins.co.uk/green**

Download the audio for this book and a reading guide for parents and teachers at www.collins.co.uk/839804